4

STONE ARCH BOOKS
a capstone imprint

STONE ARCH BOOKS™

Published in 2012
A Capstone Imprint
1710 Roe Crest Drive
North Mankato, MN 56003
www.capstonepub.com

Originally published by DC Comics in the U.S. in single magazine form as Young Justice #4.

DC Comics
1700 Broadway, New York, NY 10019
A Warner Bros. Entertainment Company

Printed in the United States of America
in Brainerd, Minnesota.
032012 006672BANGF12

Cataloging-in-Publication Data is available at the Library of Congress website:
ISBN: 978-1-4342-4556-4 (library binding)

Summary: In this action-packed story, Robin, Kid Flash, and Aqualad must escape from a duo of deadly assassins. The junior heroes will need to work as a team and take on the menace of the League of Shadows at the same time!

STONE ARCH BOOKS

Ashley C. Andersen Zantop *Publisher*
Michael Dahl *Editorial Director*
Donald Lemke & Sean Tulien *Editors*
Heather Kindseth *Creative Director*
Brann Garvey *Designer*
Kathy McColley *Production Specialist*

DC COMICS

Scott Peterson & Jim Chadwick *Original U.S. Editors*
Michael McCalister *U.S. Assistant Editor*
Mike Norton *Cover Artist*

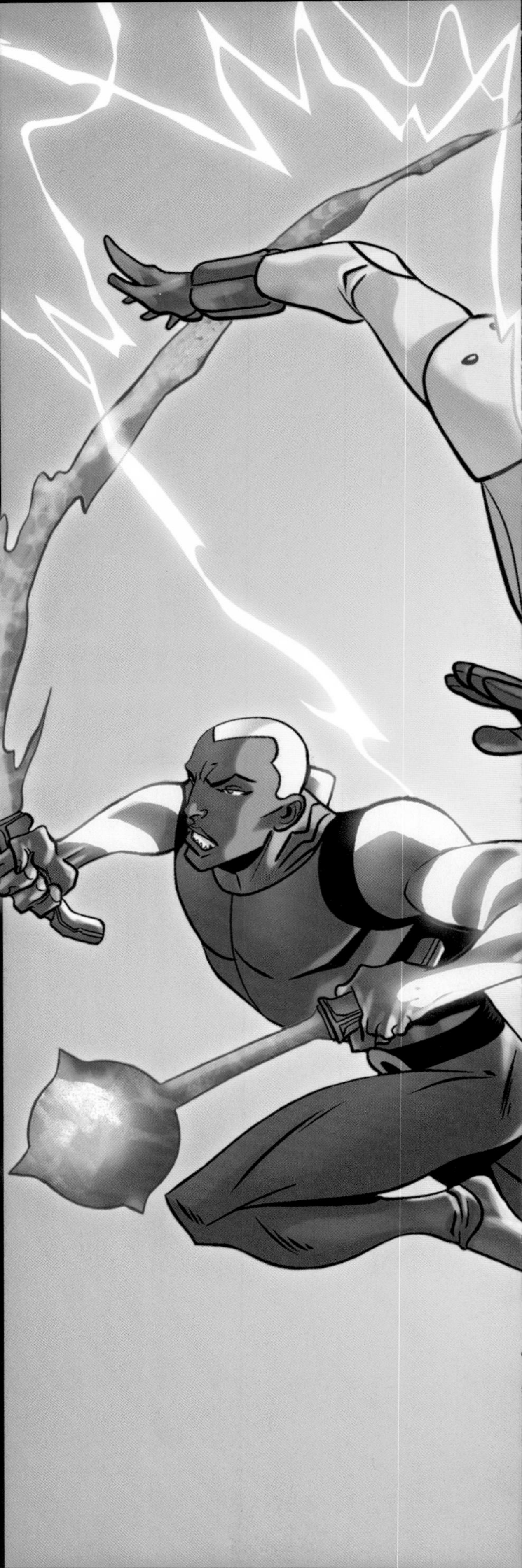

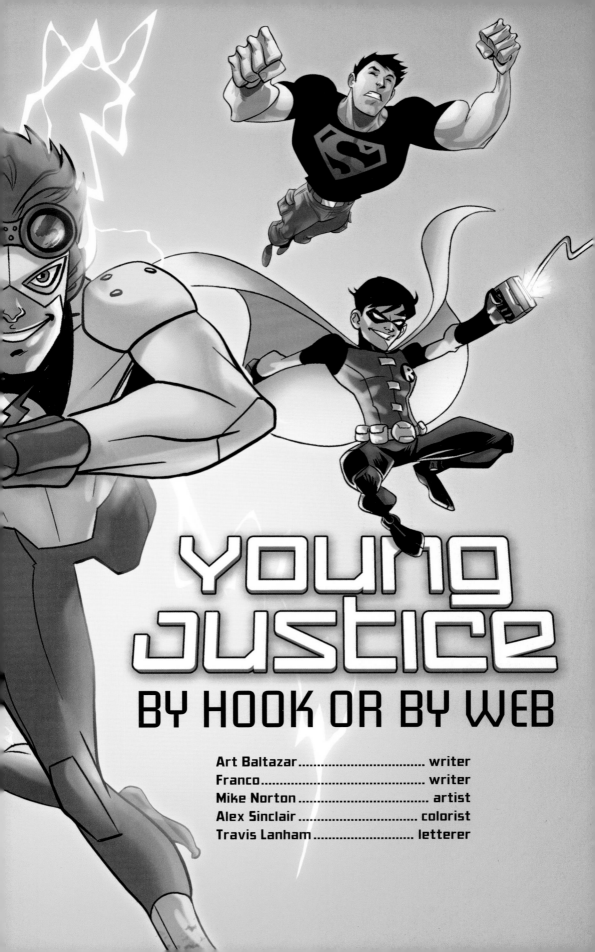

YOUNG JUSTICE

BY HOOK OR BY WEB

Art Baltazar.................................... writer
Franco.. writer
Mike Norton .... artist
Alex Sinclair .... colorist
Travis Lanham............................ letterer

YOUNG JUSTICE

AQUALAD

AGE: 16 **SECRET IDENTITY:** Kaldur' Ahm
BIO: Aquaman's apprentice; a cool, calm warrior and leader; totally amphibious with the ability to bend and shape water.

SUPERBOY

AGE: 16 **SECRET IDENTITY:** Conner Kent
BIO: Cloned from Superman; a shy and uncertain teenager; gifted with super-strength, infrared vision, and leaping abilities

ARTEMIS

AGE: 15 **SECRET IDENTITY:** Classified
BIO: Green Arrow's niece; a dedicated and tough fighter; extremely talented in both archery and martial arts.

KID FLASH

AGE: 15 **SECRET IDENTITY:** Wally West
BIO: Partner of the Flash; a competitive team member, often lacking self-control; gifted with super-speed.

ROBIN

AGE: 13 **SECRET IDENTITY:** Dick Grayson
BIO: Partner of Batman; the youngest member of the team; talented acrobat, martial artist, and hacker.

MISS MARTIAN

AGE: 16 **SECRET IDENTITY:** M'gann M'orzz
BIO: Martian Manhunter's niece; polite and sweet; ability to shape-shift, read minds, transform, and fly.

THE STORY SO FAR...

Aqualad, Kid Flash, and Robin – members of the newly formed Young Justice team – are caught in a web of trouble. While investigating the League of Shadows, a criminal organization, they are apprehended. Can the teen heroes escape these evil doers and get back on their feet...?

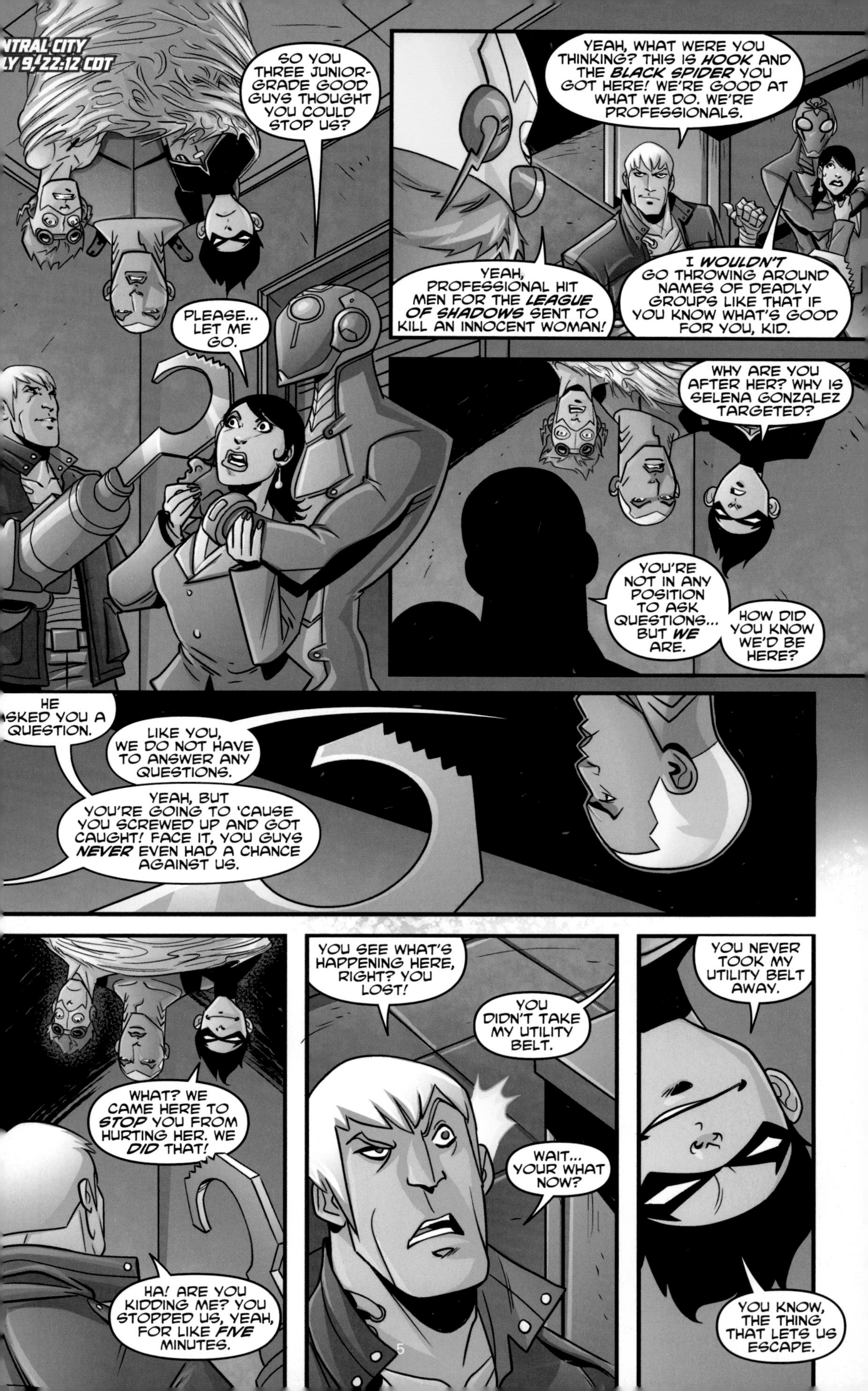

NTRAL CITY
LY 9, 22:12 CDT
SO YOU THREE JUNIOR-GRADE GOOD GUYS THOUGHT YOU COULD STOP US?
PLEASE... LET ME GO.
YEAH, WHAT WERE YOU THINKING? THIS IS HOOK AND THE BLACK SPIDER YOU GOT HERE! WE'RE GOOD AT WHAT WE DO. WE'RE PROFESSIONALS.
YEAH, PROFESSIONAL HIT MEN FOR THE LEAGUE OF SHADOWS SENT TO KILL AN INNOCENT WOMAN!
I WOULDN'T GO THROWING AROUND NAMES OF DEADLY GROUPS LIKE THAT IF YOU KNOW WHAT'S GOOD FOR YOU, KID.
WHY ARE YOU AFTER HER? WHY IS SELENA GONZALEZ TARGETED?
YOU'RE NOT IN ANY POSITION TO ASK QUESTIONS... BUT WE ARE.
HOW DID YOU KNOW WE'D BE HERE?
HE ASKED YOU A QUESTION.
LIKE YOU, WE DO NOT HAVE TO ANSWER ANY QUESTIONS.
YEAH, BUT YOU'RE GOING TO 'CAUSE YOU SCREWED UP AND GOT CAUGHT! FACE IT, YOU GUYS NEVER EVEN HAD A CHANCE AGAINST US.
WHAT? WE CAME HERE TO STOP YOU FROM HURTING HER. WE DID THAT!
HA! ARE YOU KIDDING ME? YOU STOPPED US, YEAH, FOR LIKE FIVE MINUTES.
YOU SEE WHAT'S HAPPENING HERE, RIGHT? YOU LOST!
YOU DIDN'T TAKE MY UTILITY BELT.
WAIT... YOUR WHAT NOW?
YOU NEVER TOOK MY UTILITY BELT AWAY.
YOU KNOW, THE THING THAT LETS US ESCAPE.

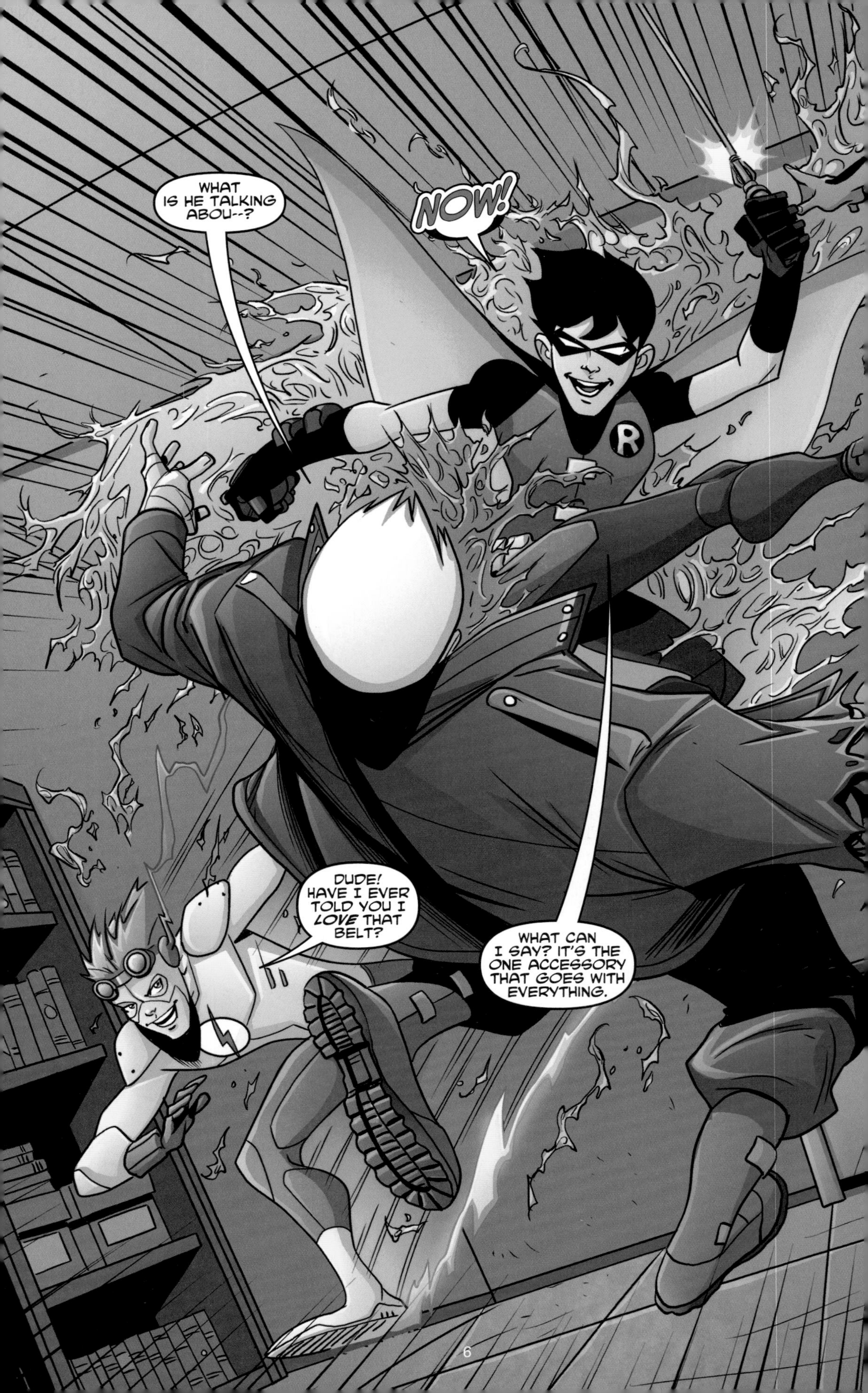
WHAT IS HE TALKING ABOU--?
NOW!
DUDE! HAVE I EVER TOLD YOU I *LOVE* THAT BELT?
WHAT CAN I SAY? IT'S THE ONE ACCESSORY THAT GOES WITH EVERYTHING.

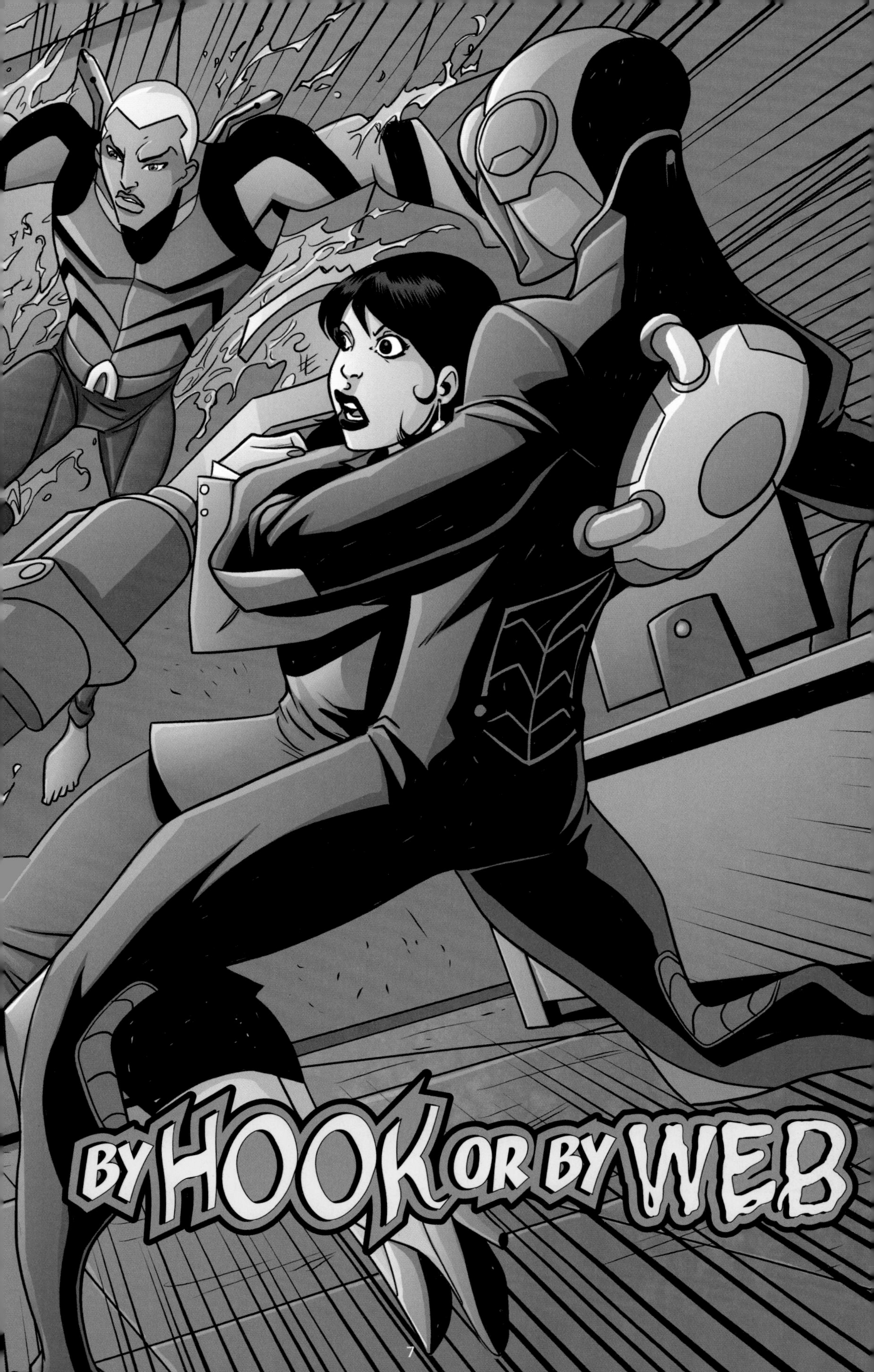
BY HOOK OR BY WEB

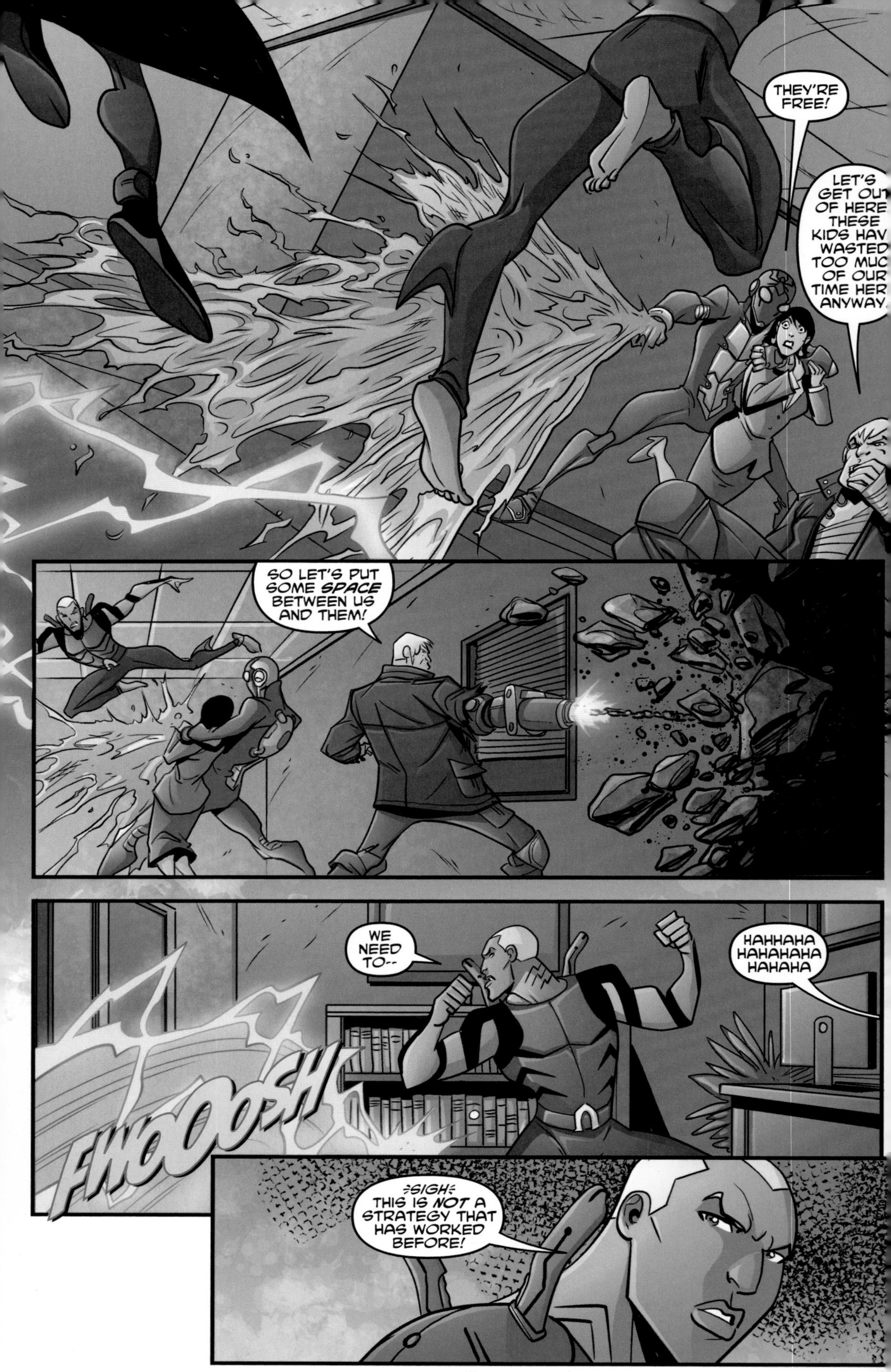

THEY'RE FREE!
LET'S GET OUT OF HERE THESE KIDS HAV WASTED TOO MUC OF OUR TIME HER ANYWAY.
SO LET'S PUT SOME SPACE BETWEEN US AND THEM!
WE NEED TO--
HAHHAHA HAHAHAHA HAHAHA
FWOOOSH
SIGH
THIS IS NOT A STRATEGY THAT HAS WORKED BEFORE!

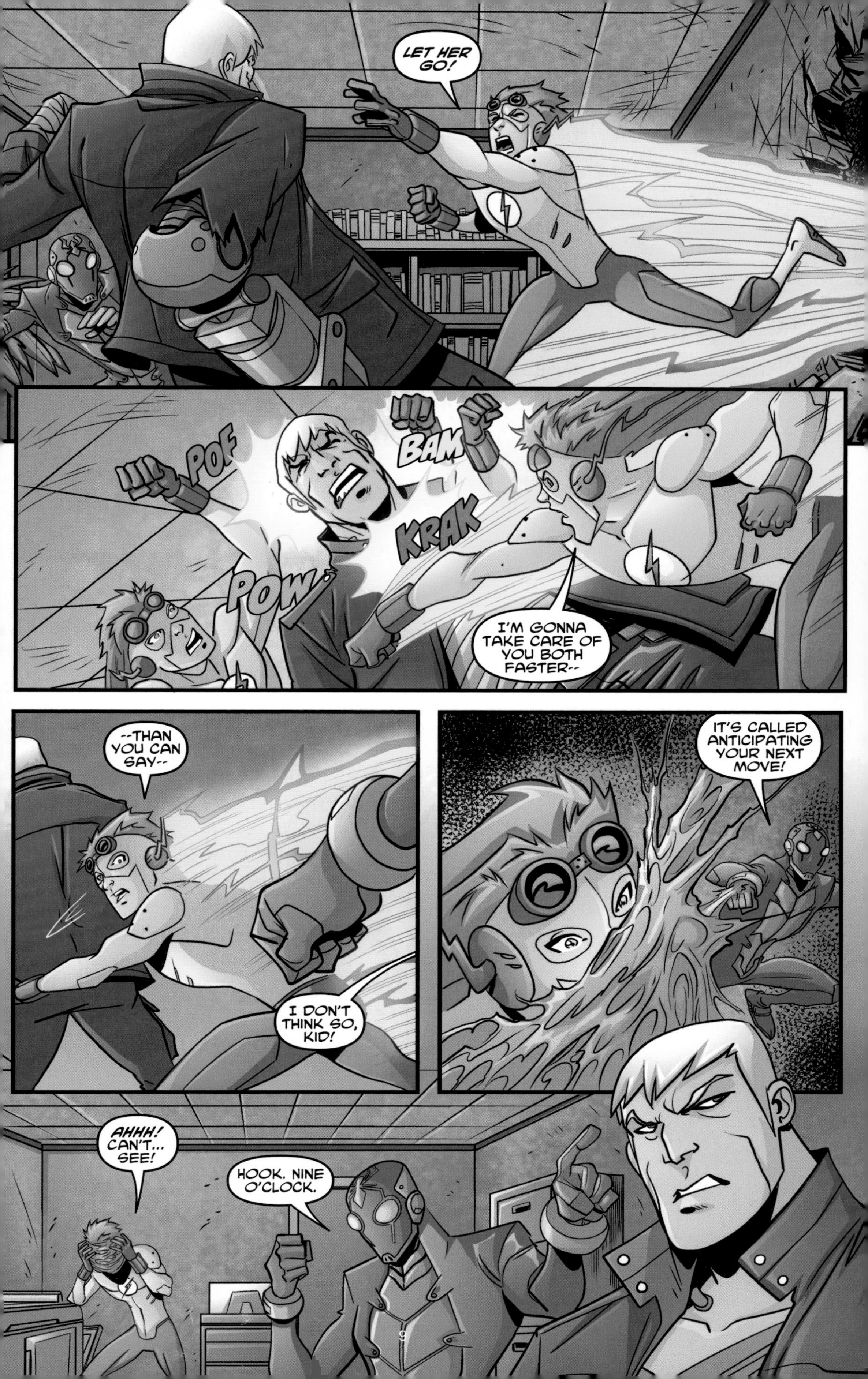
LET HER GO!
POF
BAM
KRAK
POW
I'M GONNA TAKE CARE OF YOU BOTH FASTER--
--THAN YOU CAN SAY--
I DON'T THINK SO, KID!
IT'S CALLED ANTICIPATING YOUR NEXT MOVE!
AHHH! CAN'T... SEE!
HOOK. NINE O'CLOCK.

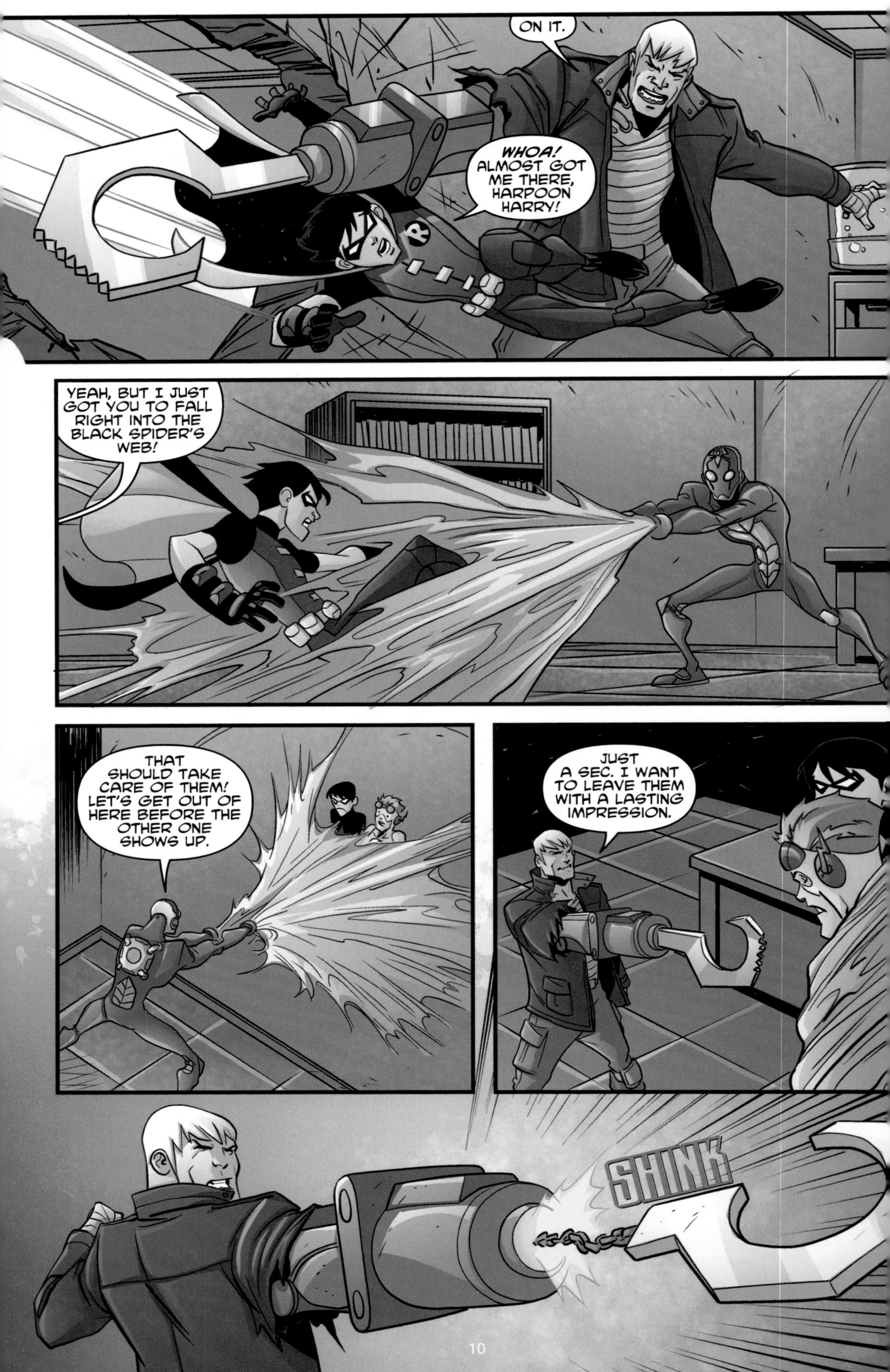
ON IT.
WHOA! ALMOST GOT ME THERE, HARPOON HARRY!
YEAH, BUT I JUST GOT YOU TO FALL RIGHT INTO THE BLACK SPIDER'S WEB!
THAT SHOULD TAKE CARE OF THEM! LET'S GET OUT OF HERE BEFORE THE OTHER ONE SHOWS UP.
JUST A SEC. I WANT TO LEAVE THEM WITH A LASTING IMPRESSION.
SHINK

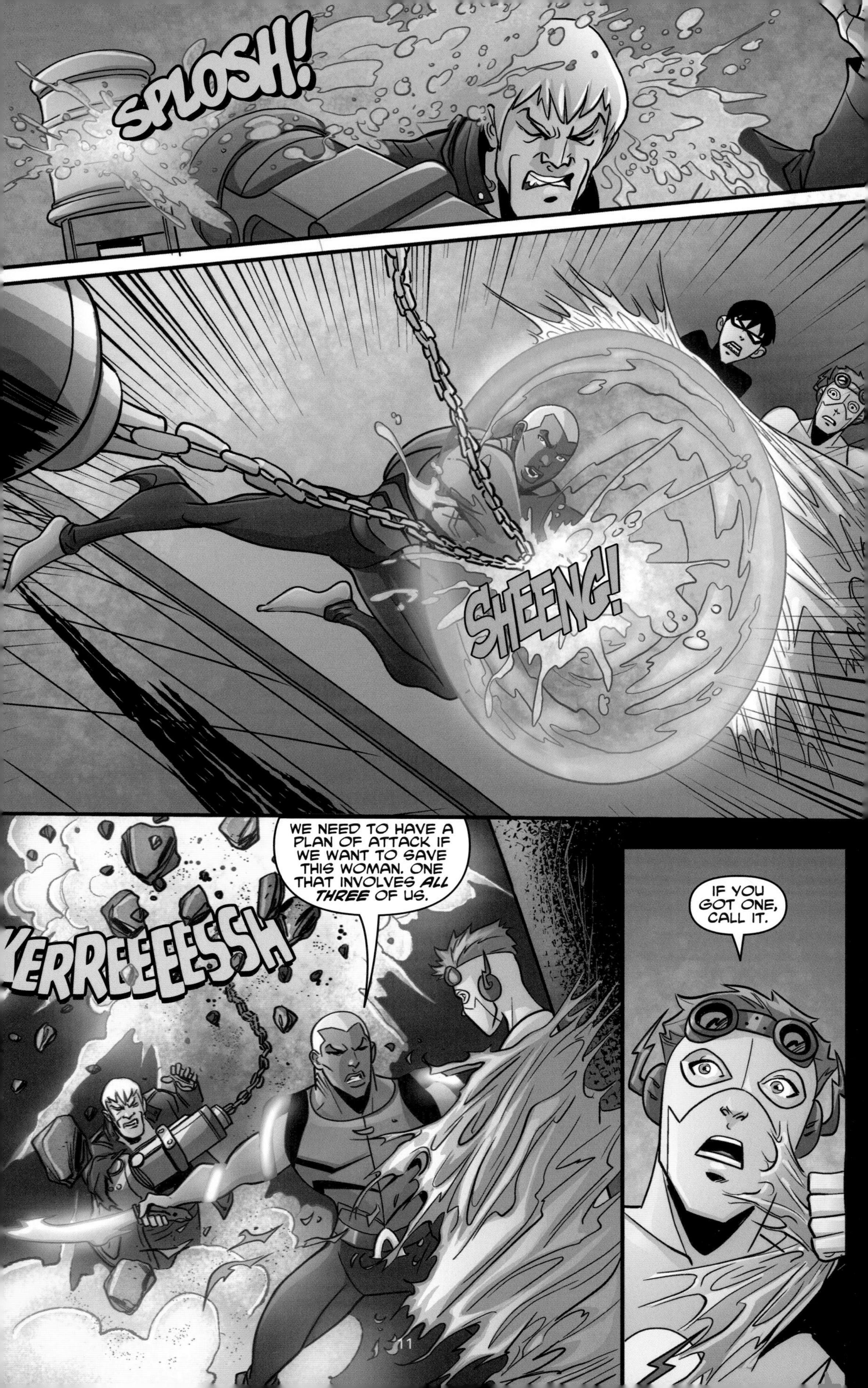
SPLOSH!
SHEENG!
KERREEEEESSH
WE NEED TO HAVE A PLAN OF ATTACK IF WE WANT TO SAVE THIS WOMAN. ONE THAT INVOLVES ALL THREE OF US.
IF YOU GOT ONE, CALL IT.

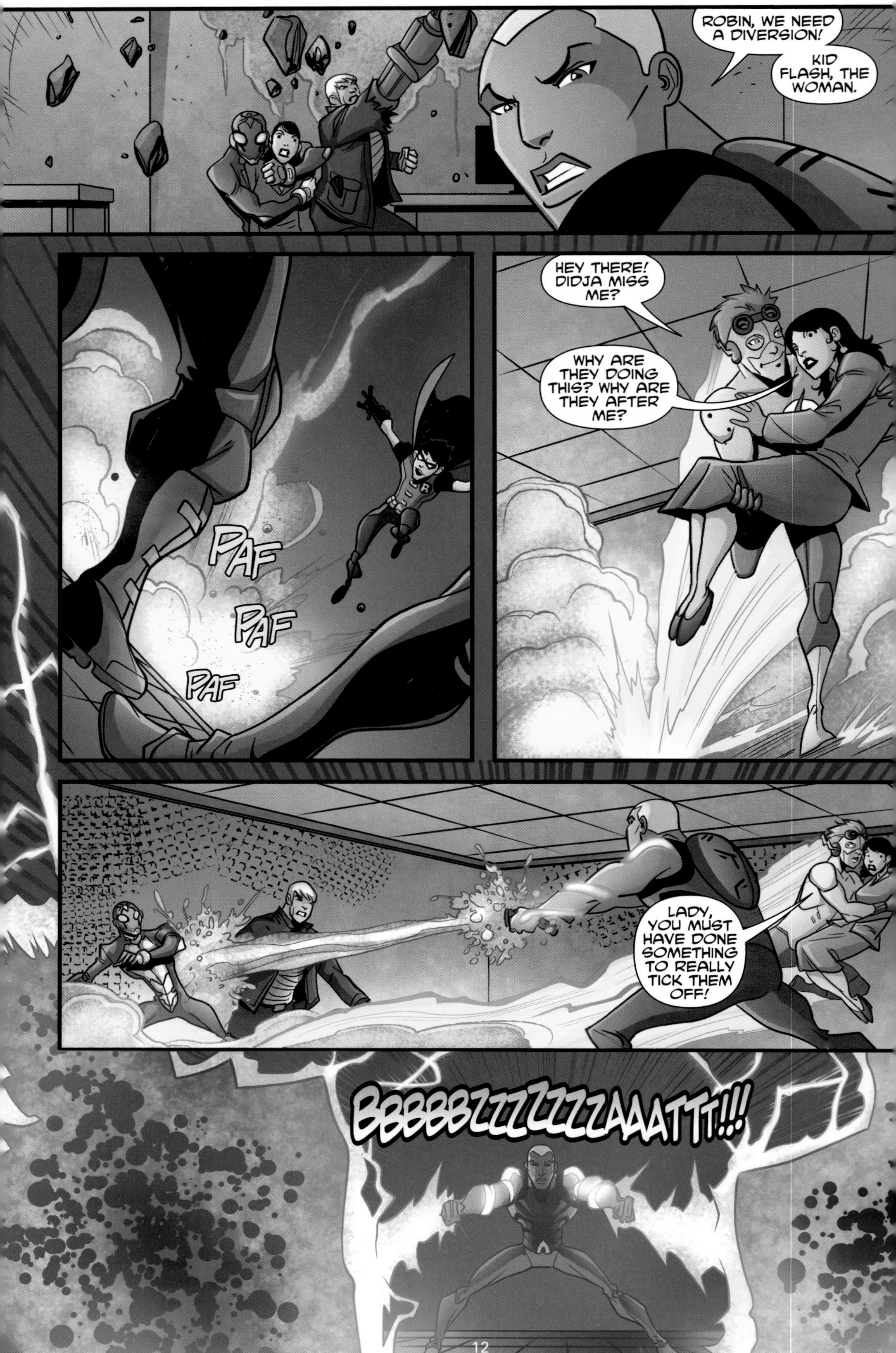
ROBIN, WE NEED A DIVERSION!
KID FLASH, THE WOMAN.
PAF
PAF
PAF
HEY THERE! DIDJA MISS ME?
WHY ARE THEY DOING THIS? WHY ARE THEY AFTER ME?
LADY, YOU MUST HAVE DONE SOMETHING TO REALLY TICK THEM OFF!
BBBBBZZZZZZZAAATTT!!!

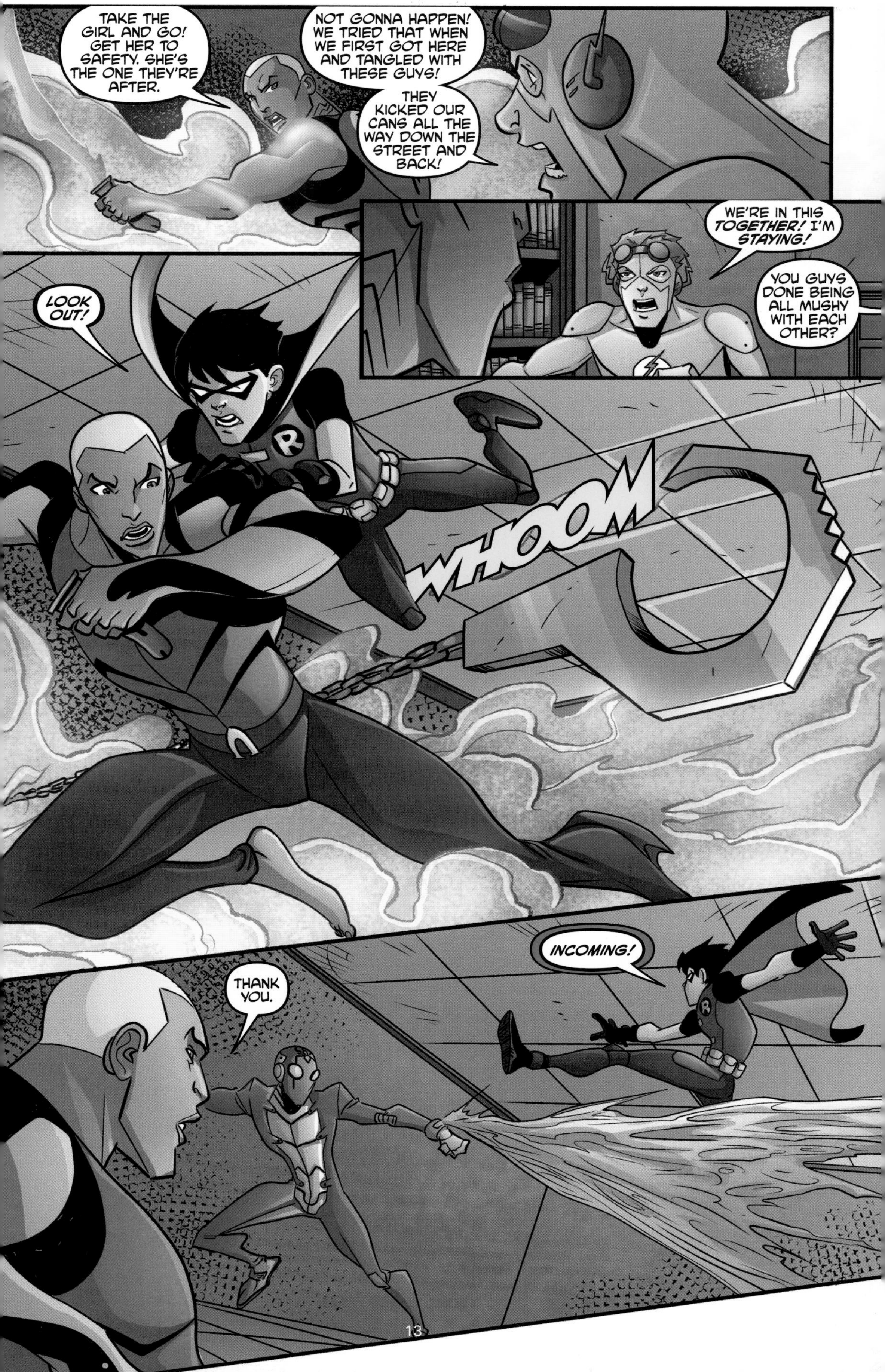
TAKE THE GIRL AND GO! GET HER TO SAFETY. SHE'S THE ONE THEY'RE AFTER.
NOT GONNA HAPPEN! WE TRIED THAT WHEN WE FIRST GOT HERE AND TANGLED WITH THESE GUYS!
THEY KICKED OUR CANS ALL THE WAY DOWN THE STREET AND BACK!
WE'RE IN THIS TOGETHER! I'M STAYING!
YOU GUYS DONE BEING ALL MUSHY WITH EACH OTHER?
LOOK OUT!
WHOOM
INCOMING!
THANK YOU.

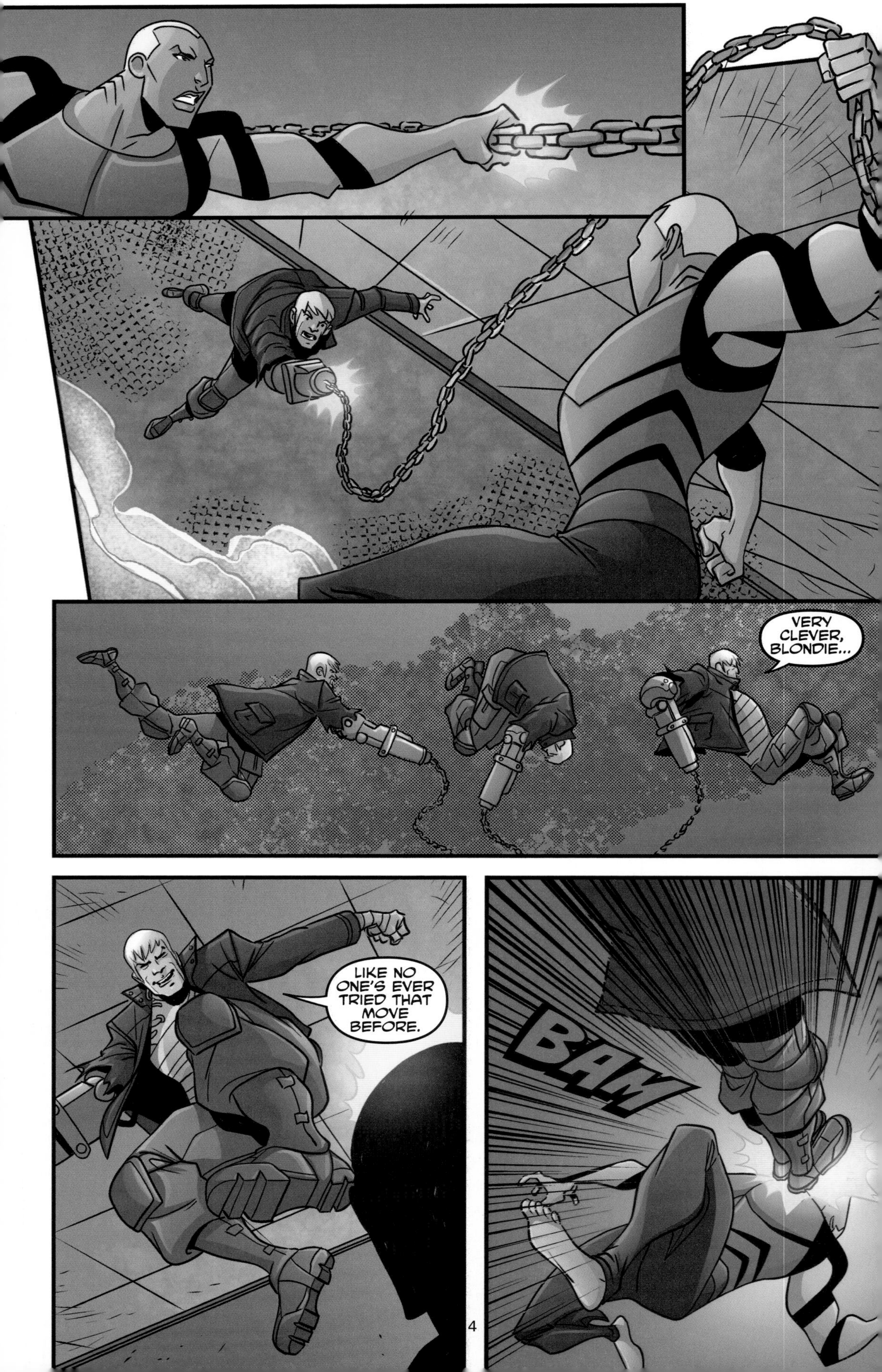
VERY CLEVER, BLONDIE...
LIKE NO ONE'S EVER TRIED THAT MOVE BEFORE.
BAM

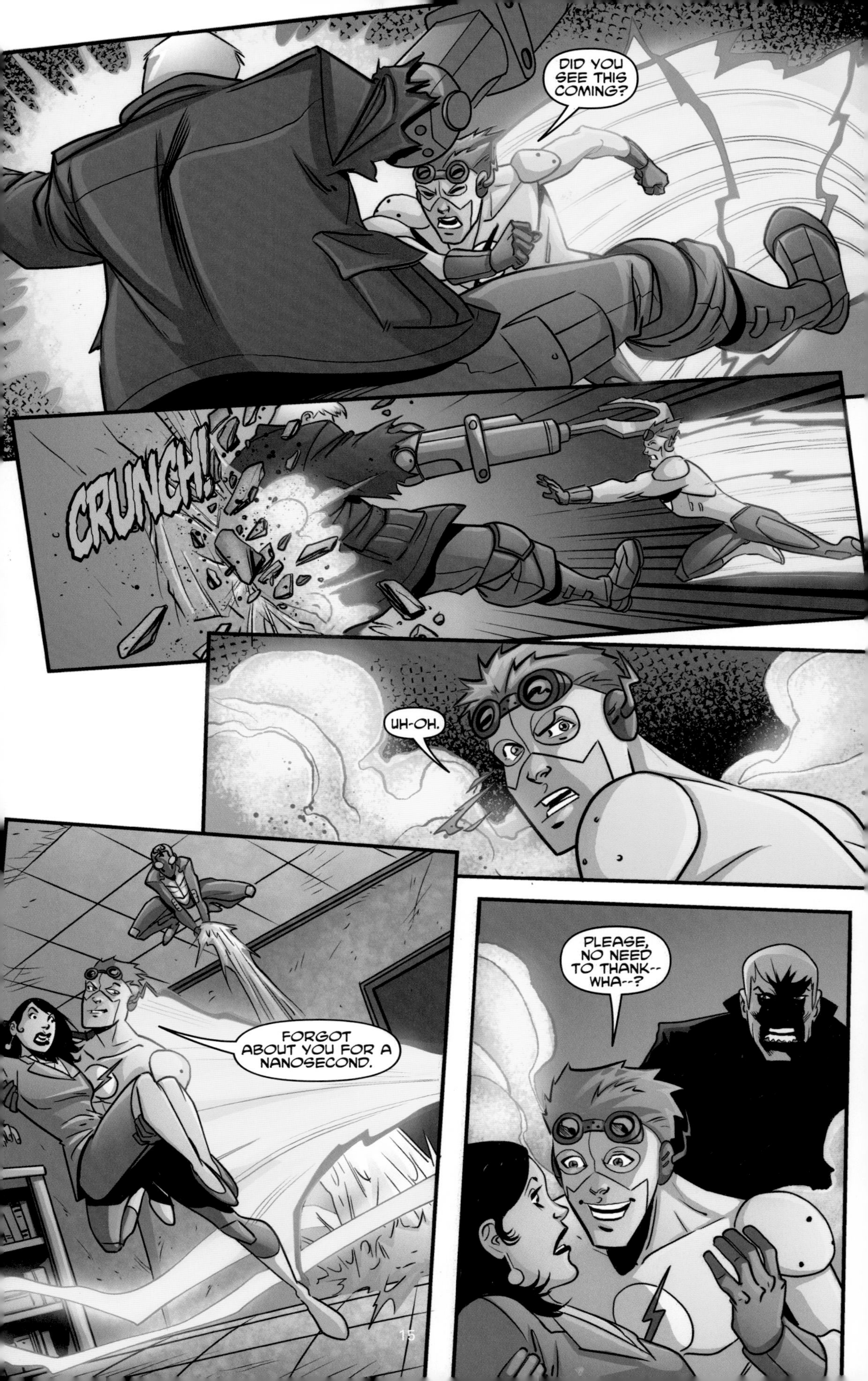
DID YOU SEE THIS COMING?
CRUNCH!
UH-OH.
FORGOT ABOUT YOU FOR A NANOSECOND.
PLEASE, NO NEED TO THANK-- WHA--?

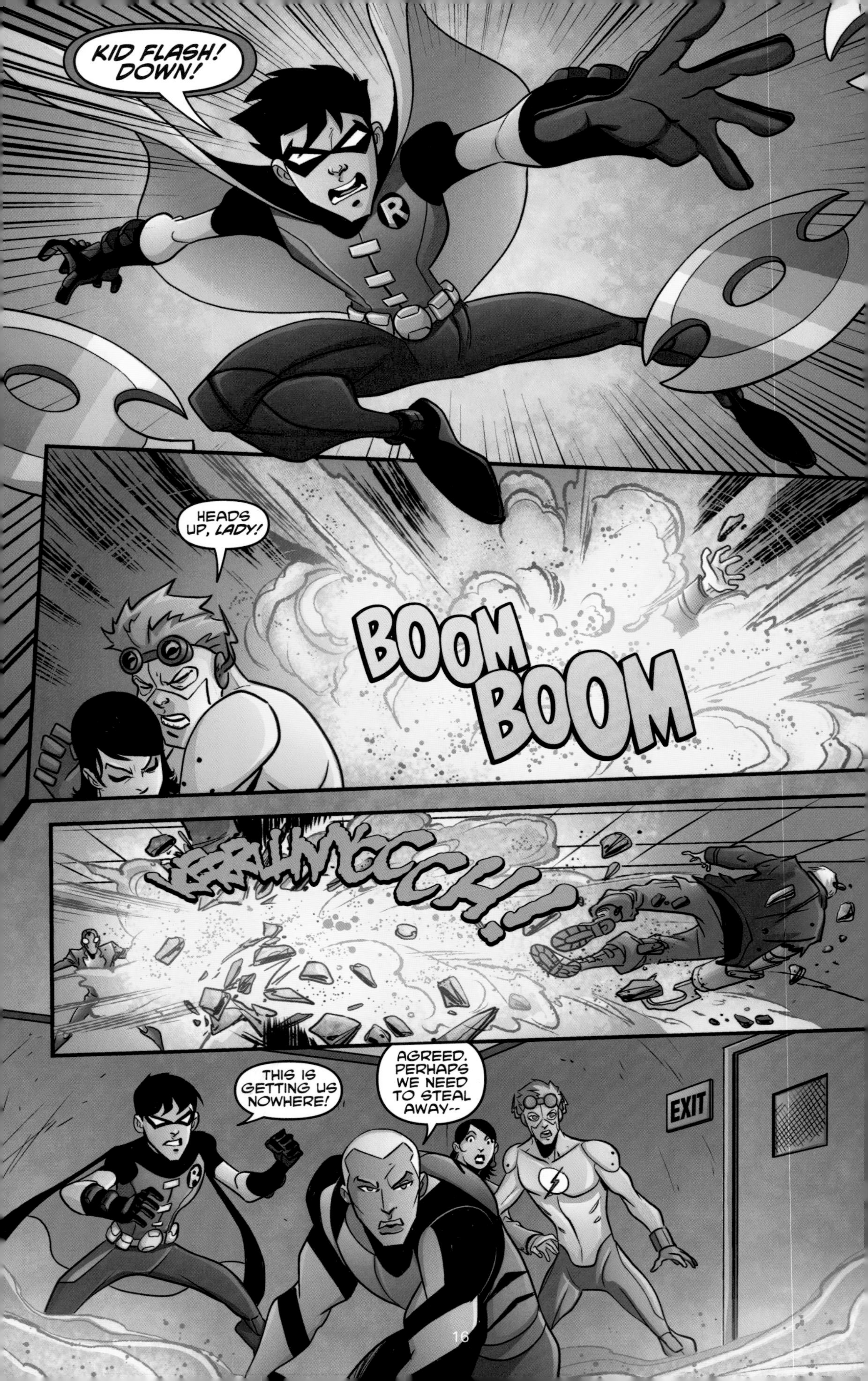
KID FLASH! DOWN!
HEADS UP, LADY!
BOOM BOOM
THIS IS GETTING US NOWHERE!
AGREED. PERHAPS WE NEED TO STEAL AWAY--
EXIT

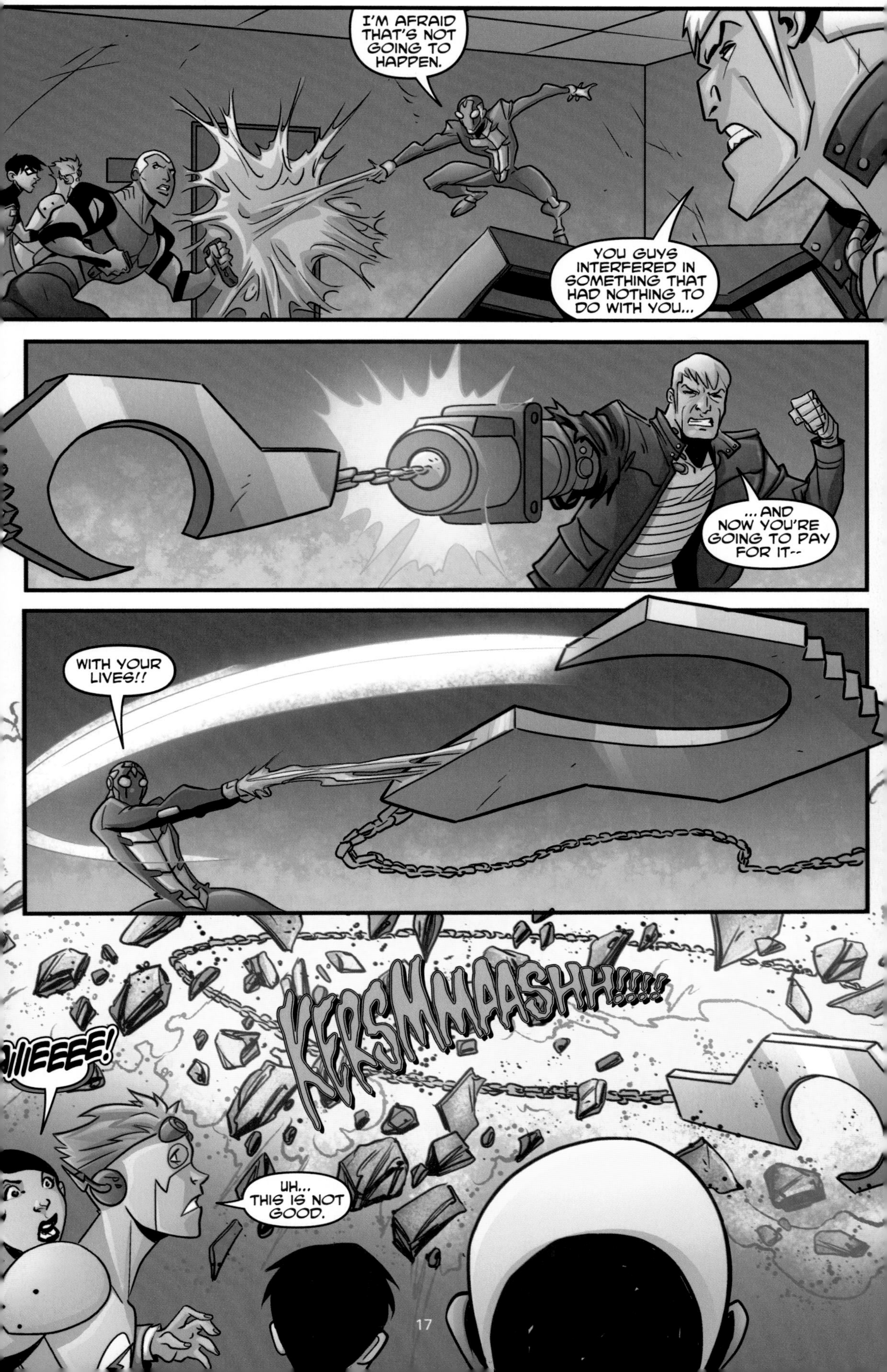

I'M AFRAID THAT'S NOT GOING TO HAPPEN.
YOU GUYS INTERFERED IN SOMETHING THAT HAD NOTHING TO DO WITH YOU...
...AND NOW YOU'RE GOING TO PAY FOR IT--
WITH YOUR LIVES!!
KERSMMAASHH!!!!!
IIIEEEEE!
UH... THIS IS NOT GOOD.

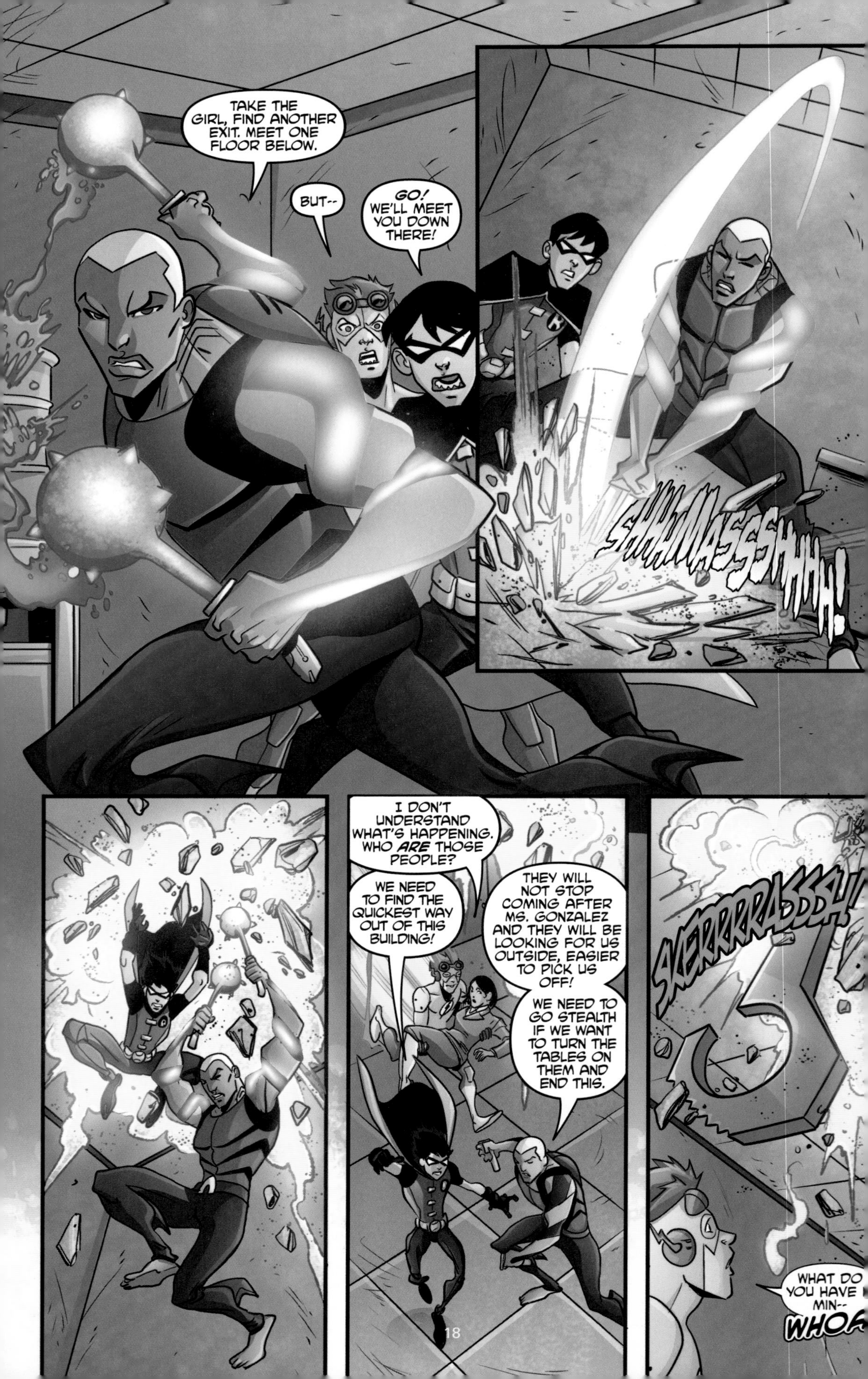
TAKE THE GIRL, FIND ANOTHER EXIT. MEET ONE FLOOR BELOW.
BUT--
GO! WE'LL MEET YOU DOWN THERE!
SHHHMASSSHHHH!
I DON'T UNDERSTAND WHAT'S HAPPENING. WHO ARE THOSE PEOPLE?
WE NEED TO FIND THE QUICKEST WAY OUT OF THIS BUILDING!
THEY WILL NOT STOP COMING AFTER MS. GONZALEZ AND THEY WILL BE LOOKING FOR US OUTSIDE, EASIER TO PICK US OFF!
WE NEED TO GO STEALTH IF WE WANT TO TURN THE TABLES ON THEM AND END THIS.
SKERRRRASSSH!
WHAT DO YOU HAVE MIN--
WHOA

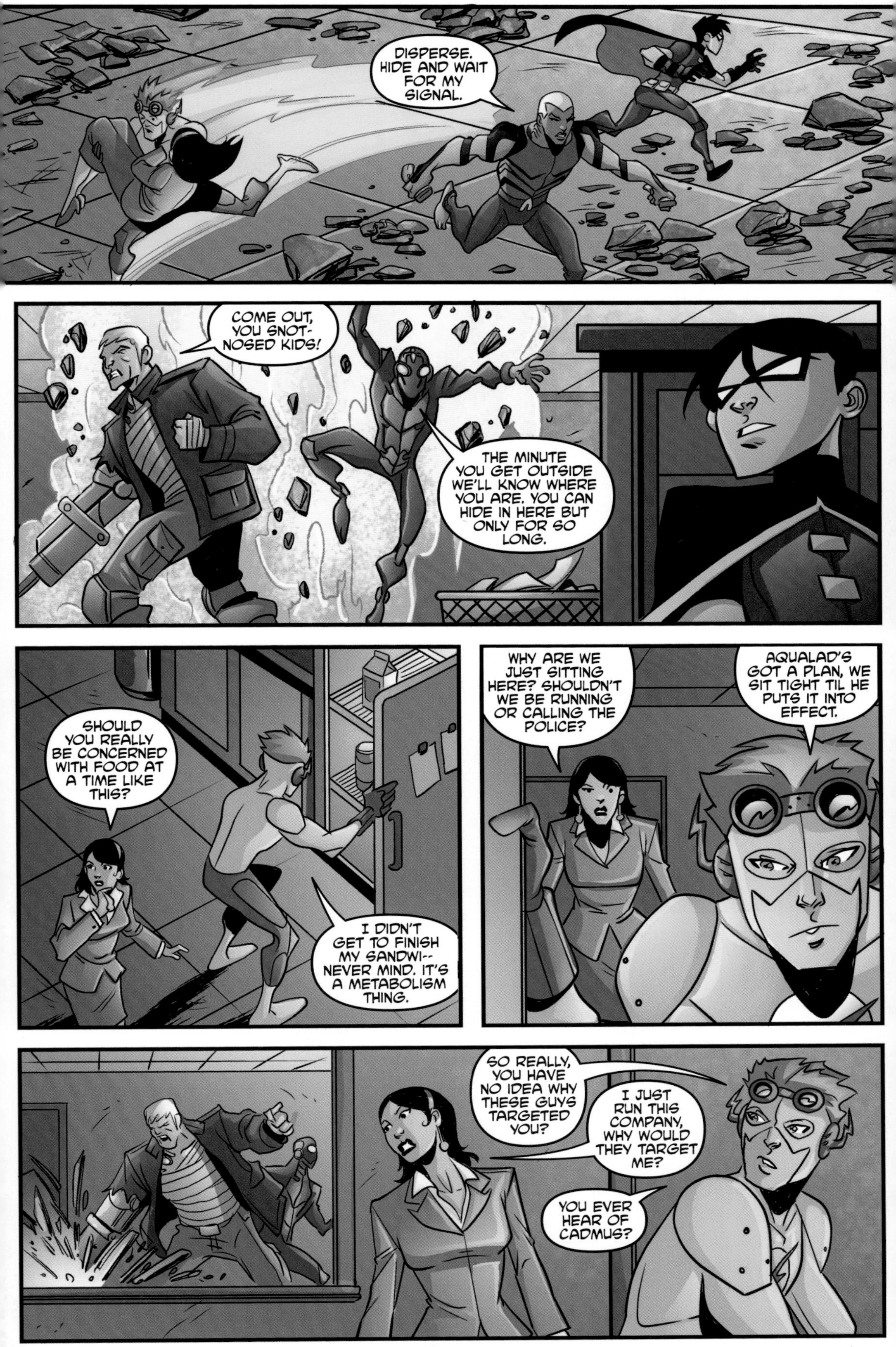
DISPERSE. HIDE AND WAIT FOR MY SIGNAL.
COME OUT, YOU SNOT-NOSED KIDS!
THE MINUTE YOU GET OUTSIDE WE'LL KNOW WHERE YOU ARE. YOU CAN HIDE IN HERE BUT ONLY FOR SO LONG.
SHOULD YOU REALLY BE CONCERNED WITH FOOD AT A TIME LIKE THIS?
I DIDN'T GET TO FINISH MY SANDWI-- NEVER MIND. IT'S A METABOLISM THING.
WHY ARE WE JUST SITTING HERE? SHOULDN'T WE BE RUNNING OR CALLING THE POLICE?
AQUALAD'S GOT A PLAN, WE SIT TIGHT TIL HE PUTS IT INTO EFFECT.
SO REALLY, YOU HAVE NO IDEA WHY THESE GUYS TARGETED YOU?
I JUST RUN THIS COMPANY, WHY WOULD THEY TARGET ME?
YOU EVER HEAR OF CADMUS?

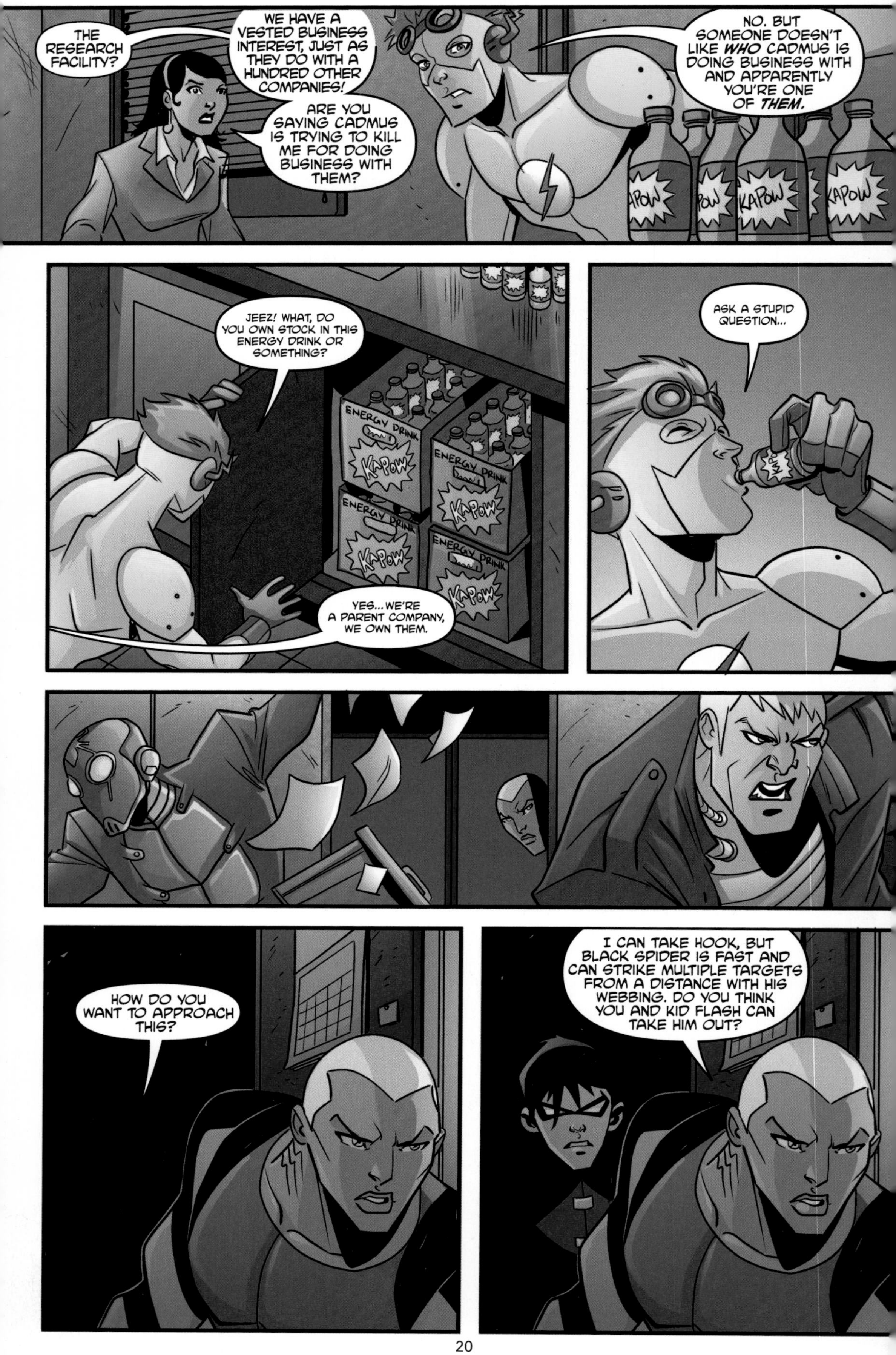
THE RESEARCH FACILITY?
WE HAVE A VESTED BUSINESS INTEREST, JUST AS THEY DO WITH A HUNDRED OTHER COMPANIES!
ARE YOU SAYING CADMUS IS TRYING TO KILL ME FOR DOING BUSINESS WITH THEM?
NO. BUT SOMEONE DOESN'T LIKE *WHO* CADMUS IS DOING BUSINESS WITH AND APPARENTLY YOU'RE ONE OF *THEM.*
KAPOW
KAPOW
KAPOW
KAPOW
JEEZ! WHAT, DO YOU OWN STOCK IN THIS ENERGY DRINK OR SOMETHING?
ENERGY DRINK
KAPOW
ENERGY DRINK
KAPOW
ENERGY DRINK
KAPOW
ENERGY DRINK
KAPOW
YES... WE'RE A PARENT COMPANY, WE OWN THEM.
ASK A STUPID QUESTION...
HOW DO YOU WANT TO APPROACH THIS?
I CAN TAKE HOOK, BUT BLACK SPIDER IS FAST AND CAN STRIKE MULTIPLE TARGETS FROM A DISTANCE WITH HIS WEBBING. DO YOU THINK YOU AND KID FLASH CAN TAKE HIM OUT?

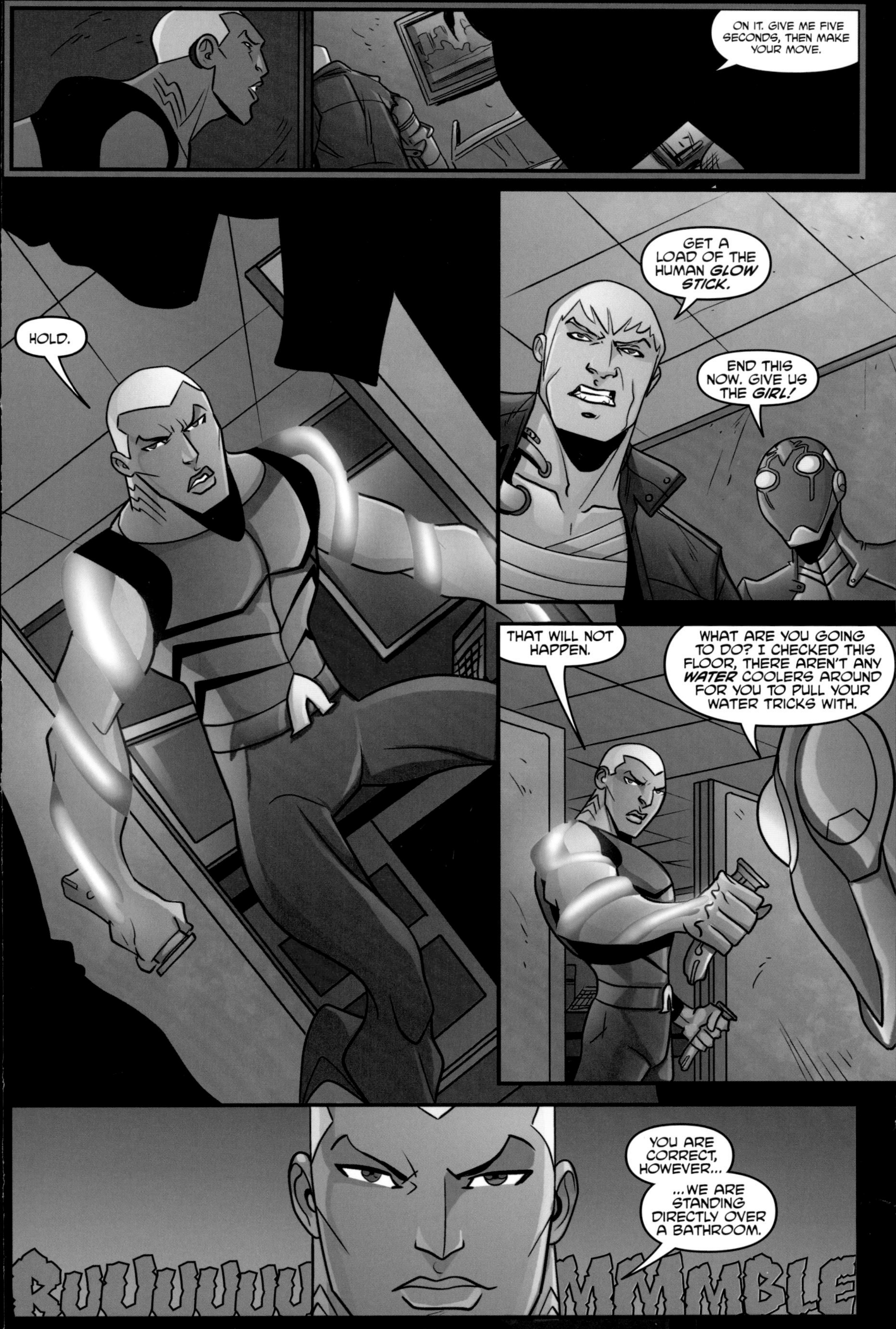

ON IT. GIVE ME FIVE SECONDS, THEN MAKE YOUR MOVE.
HOLD.
GET A LOAD OF THE HUMAN GLOW STICK.
END THIS NOW. GIVE US THE GIRL!
THAT WILL NOT HAPPEN.
WHAT ARE YOU GOING TO DO? I CHECKED THIS FLOOR, THERE AREN'T ANY WATER COOLERS AROUND FOR YOU TO PULL YOUR WATER TRICKS WITH.
YOU ARE CORRECT, HOWEVER...
...WE ARE STANDING DIRECTLY OVER A BATHROOM.
RUUUUUU...MMMBLE

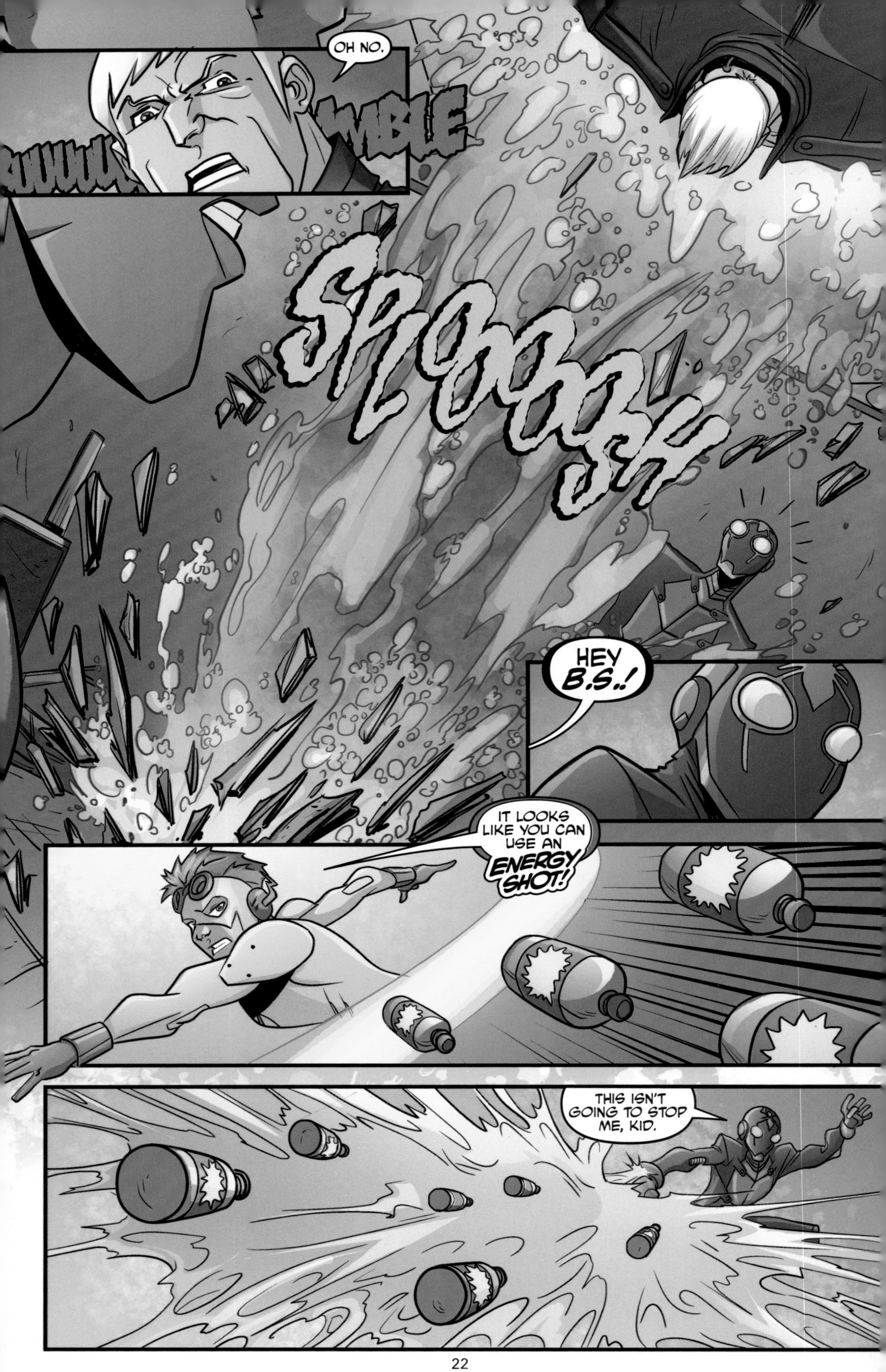
OH NO.
RUMBLE
SPLOOOSH!
HEY B.S.!
IT LOOKS LIKE YOU CAN USE AN ENERGY SHOT!
THIS ISN'T GOING TO STOP ME, KID.

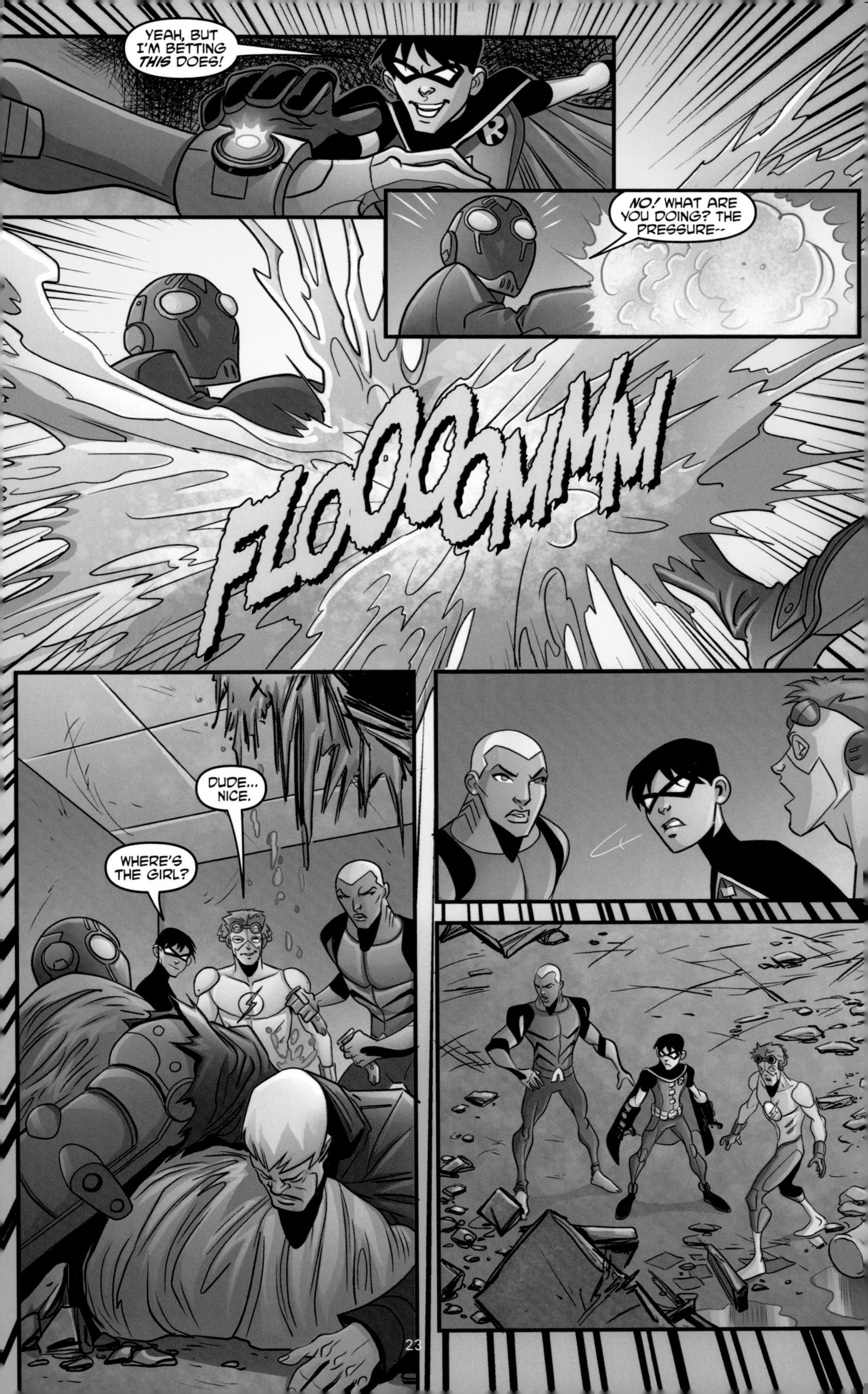

YEAH, BUT I'M BETTING *THIS* DOES!
NO! WHAT ARE YOU DOING? THE PRESSURE--
FZLOOOOMMMM
DUDE... NICE.
WHERE'S THE GIRL?

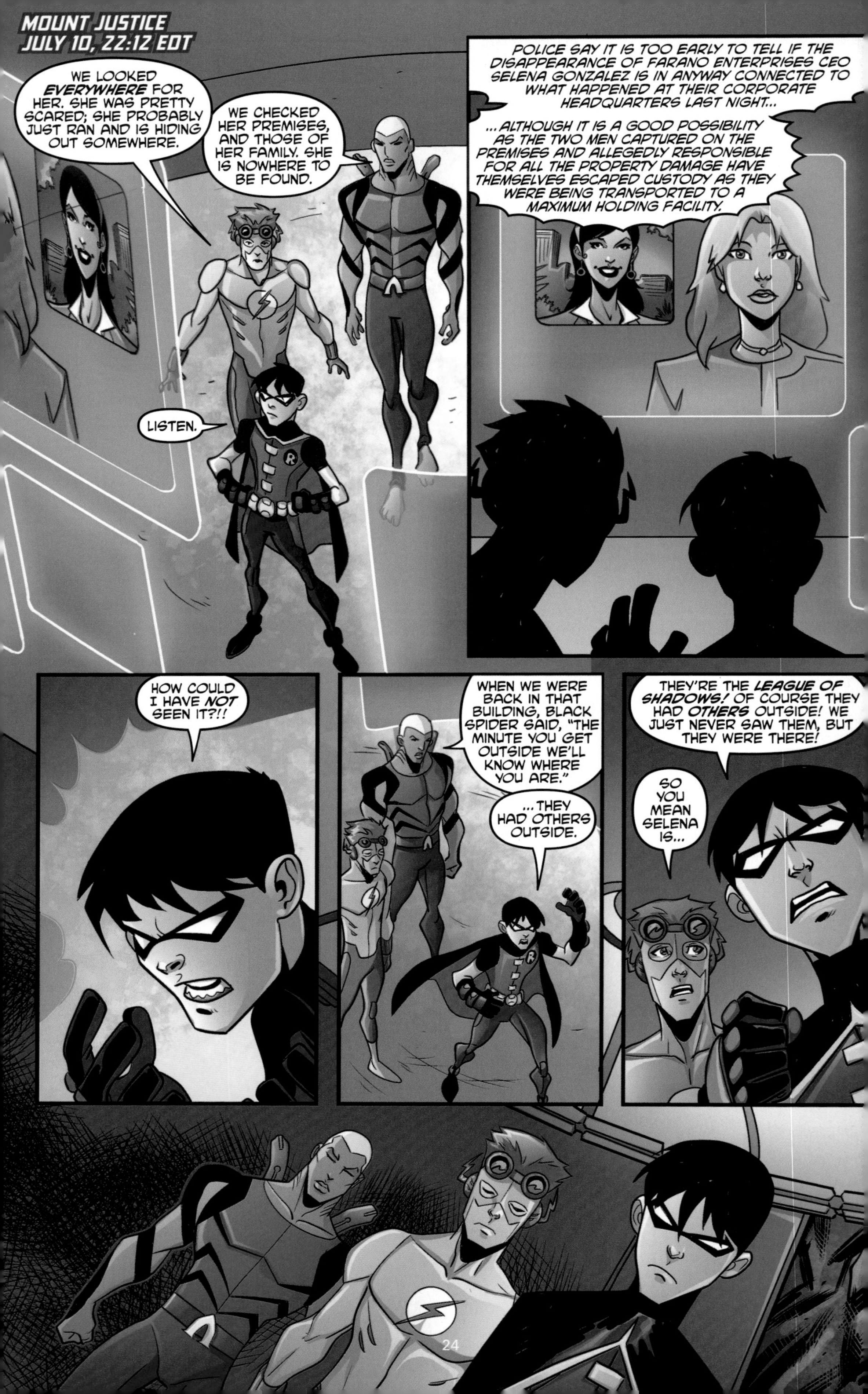
MOUNT JUSTICE
JULY 10, 22:12 EDT
WE LOOKED EVERYWHERE FOR HER. SHE WAS PRETTY SCARED; SHE PROBABLY JUST RAN AND IS HIDING OUT SOMEWHERE.
WE CHECKED HER PREMISES, AND THOSE OF HER FAMILY. SHE IS NOWHERE TO BE FOUND.
LISTEN.
POLICE SAY IT IS TOO EARLY TO TELL IF THE DISAPPEARANCE OF FARANO ENTERPRISES CEO SELENA GONZALEZ IS IN ANYWAY CONNECTED TO WHAT HAPPENED AT THEIR CORPORATE HEADQUARTERS LAST NIGHT...
...ALTHOUGH IT IS A GOOD POSSIBILITY AS THE TWO MEN CAPTURED ON THE PREMISES AND ALLEGEDLY RESPONSIBLE FOR ALL THE PROPERTY DAMAGE HAVE THEMSELVES ESCAPED CUSTODY AS THEY WERE BEING TRANSPORTED TO A MAXIMUM HOLDING FACILITY.
HOW COULD I HAVE NOT SEEN IT?!!
WHEN WE WERE BACK IN THAT BUILDING, BLACK SPIDER SAID, "THE MINUTE YOU GET OUTSIDE WE'LL KNOW WHERE YOU ARE."
...THEY HAD OTHERS OUTSIDE.
THEY'RE THE LEAGUE OF SHADOWS! OF COURSE THEY HAD OTHERS OUTSIDE! WE JUST NEVER SAW THEM, BUT THEY WERE THERE!
SO YOU MEAN SELENA IS...

CAN YOUNG JUSTICE TURN THINGS AROUND...?

Read the next action-packed adventure to find out!

only from...

STONE ARCH BOOKS™

a capstone imprint www.capstonepub.com

CREATORS

ART BALTAZAR WRITER

Art Baltazar is a cartoonist machine from the heart of Chicago! He defines cartoons and comics not only as an art style, but as a way of life. Currently, Art is the creative force behind *The New York Times* best-selling, Eisner Award-winning, DC Comics series Tiny Titans, and the co-writer for Billy Batson and the Magic of SHAZAM! and co-creator of Superman Family Adventures. Art is living the dream! He draws comics and never has to leave the house. He lives with his lovely wife, Rose, big boy Sonny, little boy Gordon, and little girl Audrey. Right on!

FRANCO AURELIANI WRITER

Bronx, New York born writer and artist Franco Aureliani has been drawing comics since he could hold a crayon. Currently residing in upstate New York with his wife, Ivette, and son, Nicolas, Franco spends most of his days in a Batcave-like studio where he produces DC's Tiny Titans comics. In 1995, Franco founded Blindwolf Studios, an independent art studio where he and fellow creators can create children's comics. Franco is the creator, artist, and writer of Weirdsville, L'il Creeps, and Eagle All Star, as well as the co-creator and writer of Patrick the Wolf Boy. When he's not writing and drawing, Franco also teaches high school art.

MIKE NORTON ARTIST

Mike Norton has been a professional comic book artist for more than ten years. His best-known works for DC Comics include the series Young Justice, All-New Atom, and Green Arrow/Black Canary.

GLOSSARY

accessory (ak-SESS-uh-ree)--something like a belt or scarf that goes with your clothes

anticipating (an-TISS-uh-pay-ting)--expecting something to happen and being prepared for it

clever (KLEV-ur)--able to understand or do things quickly and easily

disperse (diss-PURSS)--scatter

diversion (duh-VUR-zhuhn)--something that takes your mind off other things

facility (fuh-SIL-uh-tee)--a building or site used for a specific purpose

harming (HARM-ing)--injuring or hurting someone or something

interfered (in-tur-FEERD)--involved yourself in a situation that has nothing to do with you, or hindered the progress of someone or something

nanosecond (NAN-uh-sek-uhnd)--one billionth of a second

stealth (STELTH)--a person or thing regarded as a danger

vested (VESS-tid)--protected or established by law

VISUAL QUESTIONS & PROMPTS

1. Based on the illustration in the panel below, what do you think Aqualad meant when he told Kid Flash and Robin to "disperse"?

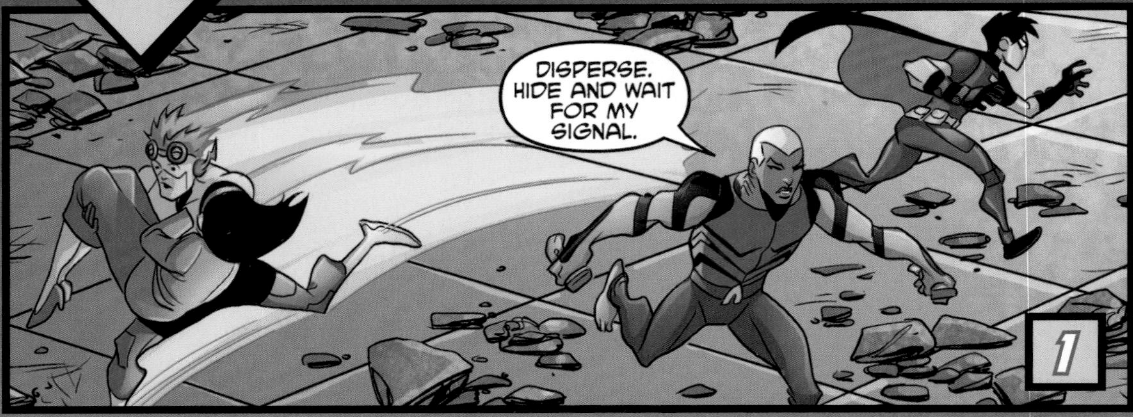
DISPERSE. HIDE AND WAIT FOR MY SIGNAL.
1

2. The panel below is the last image of these three characters in this comic book. How do you think Aqualad, Kid Flash, and Robin feel about the turn of events based on the expressions they have on their faces? Be specific.

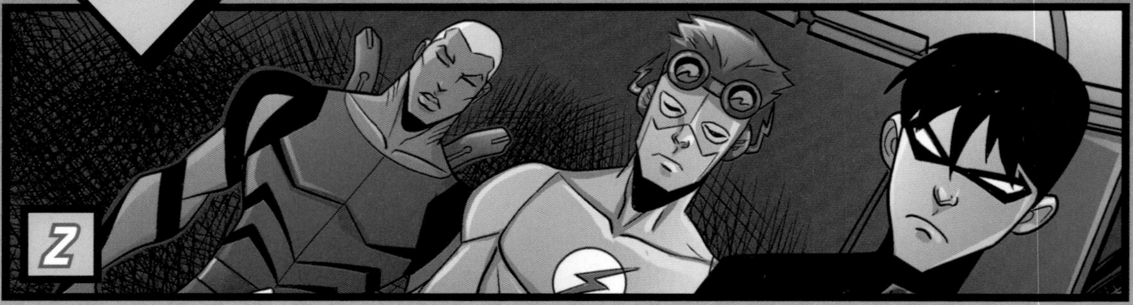
2

3. There are many ways to show movement in comic books. Do you like the way they showed this character's front flip? Why? If not, how would you have chosen to illustrate it?

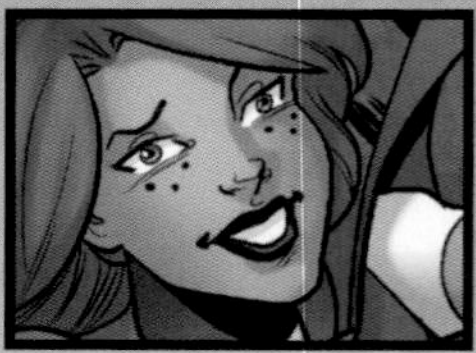

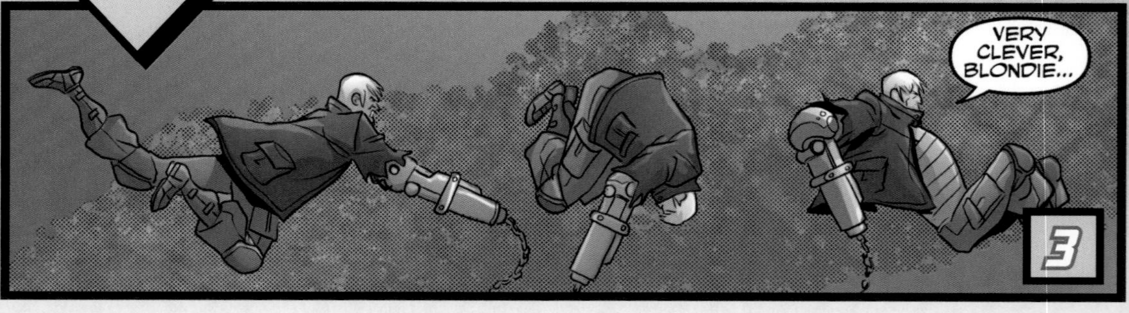
VERY CLEVER, BLONDIE...
3

YOU SEE WHAT'S HAPPENING HERE, RIGHT? YOU LOST!

YOU DIDN'T TAKE MY UTILITY BELT.

WAIT... YOUR WHAT NOW?

4.

4. Based on the dialogue present in the panel to the left, what do you think the little burst by his head means? Why?

KLICK KLICK KLICK

HEY, SUPERBOY! COME MEET MISS M.

5. In the panel to the right, Aqualad uses his superpowers to protect Kid Flash and Robin. Identify several other times in this book where one super hero or super-villain protects or helps another character.

SHEENG!

5

EXIT. MEET ONE FLOOR BELOW.

BUT--

GO! WE'LL MEET YOU DOWN THERE!

6

6. Aqualad has the ability to manipulate water and make it do whatever he wants. What other useful things could he create to help him fight crime? Write down or draw a few more ways he can use his superpower.

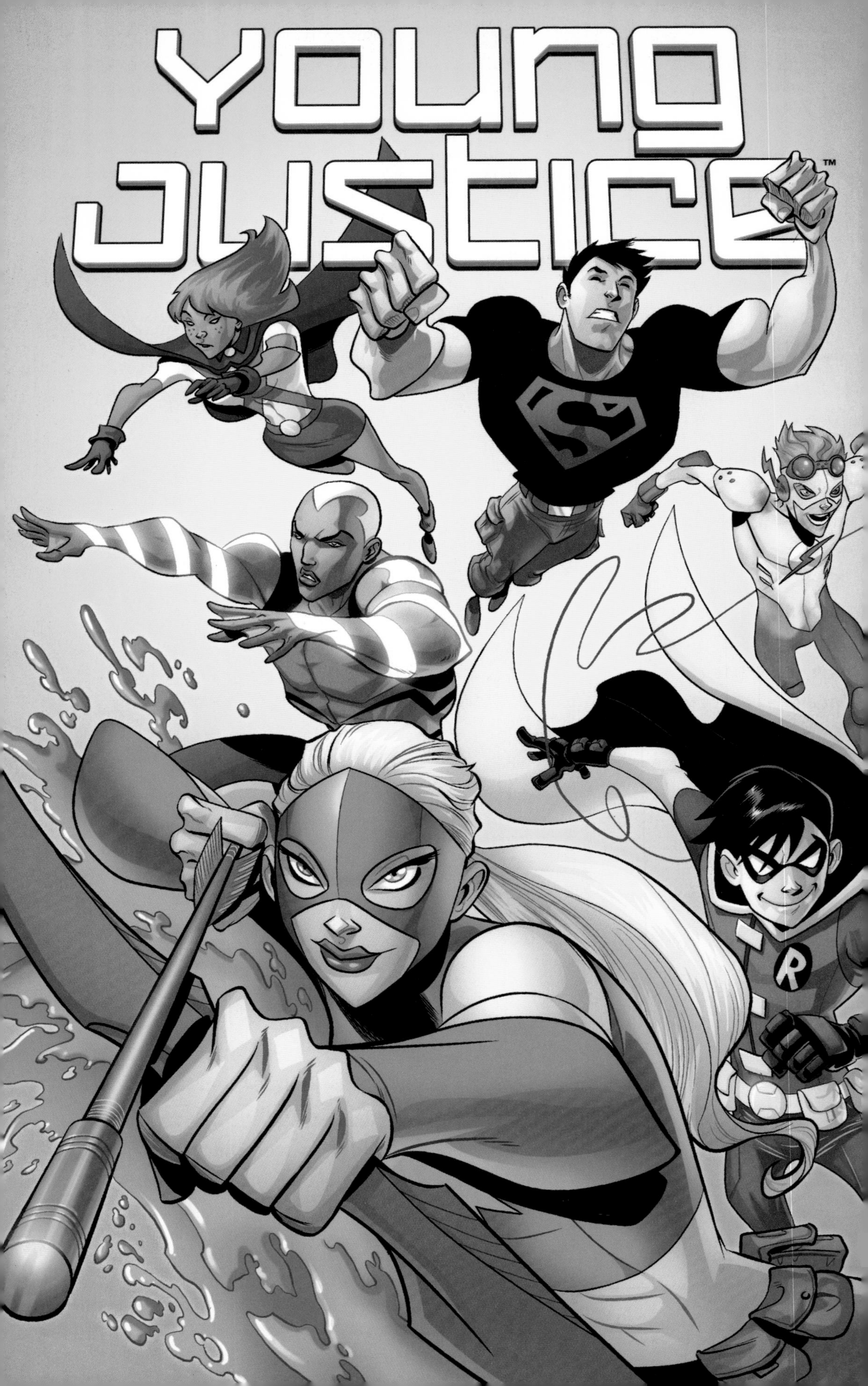
YOUNG JUSTICE™

READ THEM ALL!

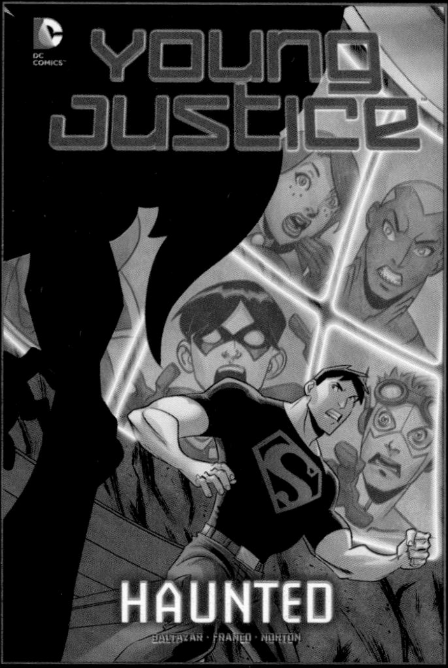
DC COMICS
YOUNG JUSTICE
HAUNTED
BALTAZAR · FRANCO · NORTON

Haunted

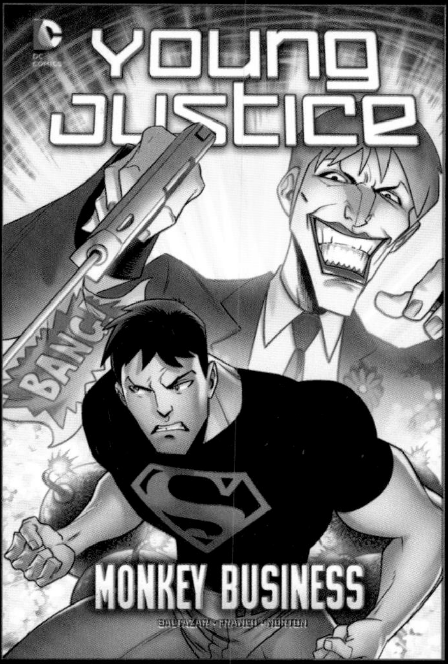
DC COMICS
YOUNG JUSTICE
BANG
MONKEY BUSINESS
BALTAZAR · FRANCO · NORTON

Monkey Business

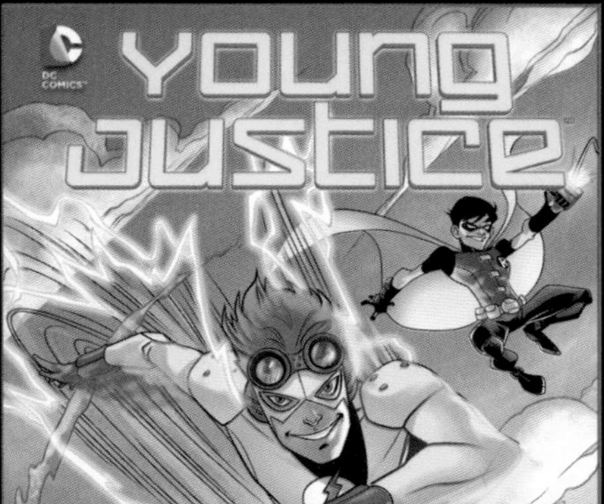
DC COMICS
YOUNG JUSTICE
HACK AND YOU SHALL FIND
BALTAZAR · FRANCO · NORTON

Hack and You Shall Find

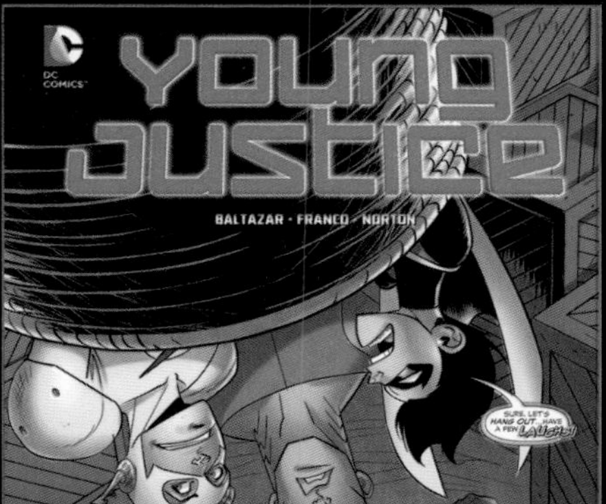
DC COMICS
YOUNG JUSTICE
BALTAZAR · FRANCO · NORTON
BY HOOK OR BY WEB

By Hook or By Web

only from...

STONE ARCH BOOKS™

a capstone imprint www.capstonepub.com

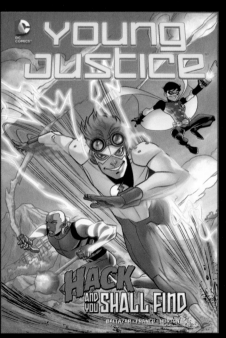

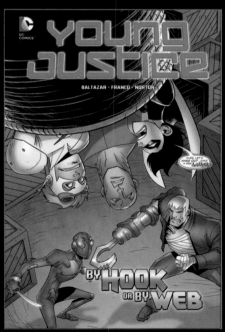

Young Justice™

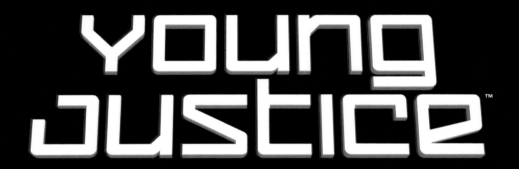